DARE TO DREAM

AADITYA MISHRA

For parents

For dreamers

For the one who dares to dream

Contents

Acknowledgements

Writing a book is never a solo activity. It takes a village for support, encouragement, and inspiration. As I write the closing words of "Dare to Dream," I'd want to offer my profound appreciation to the following:

To my parents, who taught me that dreams are worth pursuing even when the world demands practicality. To my sibling, who supported me during my late-night writing sessions and believed in my vision. To Mr. Binod Sharma, my theatre and drama teacher and National School of Drama graduate, who sparked my interest in storytelling. To the girl who defied stereotypes by wearing a saree onstage. Her fortitude served as the inspiration for this work. To the artist who sketched his dreams in private diaries. May your canvas always be vast. To the moon, stars, and guru Ji that whispered stories into my heart, to the barren corridors of my mind, where creativity bloomed. Thank you for embarking on this journey with me. Your curiosity, sensitivity, and creativity make these pages come to life.

Remember that dreams are the ink that creates our destiny. Let us continue to dream, dare, and dance amid the stars.

With deepest thanks,

Aaditya Mishra

May "Dare to Dream" encourage you to pursue your own wildest ambitions.

I
Chapter one

God shows dreams to every one of us, both good and bad. Dreams can sometimes reflect the truth of our lives, sometimes they keep coming just like that, without any strong motive. Sometimes we interpret them as unpleasant dreams or nightmares and forget about them. Still, often we get the feeling that this dream is exclusively for us, that it has a purpose and is somehow related to our life, and we begin to draw parallels between our dreams and our reality. These are the kinds of dreams that stick with us forever. When we analyze dreams with an open mind, we often discover that they reflect our real lives, even though they are difficult to explain. Through those dreams, we can achieve the objectives that we've always cherished. Moreover, we are free to pursue any idea we have while we are lost in our imagination, free from the constraints and expectations of society. Some dreams offer gifts and lessons that one will never forget.

Filtered sunshine streamed through the window, creating a pleasant environment on this magnificent day. The gentle chirping of a house sparrow enhances the magical atmosphere. Gorgeous drawings of elite clothing, posters, and pink walls beautify the room, and a wall covered with decorations is surrounded by medals and prizes. A large, black-framed poster hung on the wall in front of her. The poster featured a young woman wearing a saree and standing against the backdrop of the Himalayas.

The fifteen-year-old girl Tamanna Gupta is sleeping soundly and grinning, holding the blanket near her face as the sun shines through the curtains, giving her a moment that seems like it will never end. Tamanna glided like a whispered secret in the sun-kissed city of Ajmer, where the aroma of marigolds lingered in little lanes. Her family's house had dusty windowsills where she sketched designs with her fingertips, and her almond-shaped eyes captured the colors of dusk. But underneath her reserved exterior was a storm, a fantasy that dared not come to light. She wanted to become a famous fashion designer. Her passion was to be a top-notch designer in the industry, but her parents, who were strict and conservative, had different plans for her. Tamanna is the only child of her parents, and they expect her to carry out their duties as responsibility.

The smile is gradually starting to wane when the distant voice *"Get up, it's almost seven; you could be late."* Perhaps it was the end of this mesmerizing and attractive atmosphere at that exact time since the voice sounded terrible. Tamanna, the girl who had been dreaming and enjoying, was startled by her mother's voice and immediately woke up, then she saw her mother, who was looking at her from outside the room.

The sound of steel cookware clattering in the kitchen interrupted Tamanna's lovely moment. She was clutching a silky, smooth blanket that she was unwilling to let go of, but life marched on, and she woke up. Since Tamanna still isn't ready to get out of bed, her mother is standing at the door, peering at her and growing a bit impatient with her.

Mrs. Bharti Gupta, her strict mother, was a sensible person with a neatly tied bun. She was astonished and terrified to see her mother waiting at the door of the room when she opened her eyes. When she woke up and noticed how completely the room had changed—there were no medals, posters, or even prizes—she understood it was a dream, but before she could collect herself, her mother proceeded to open the window. The cold morning breeze rustles the papers that she left on her study desk the night before. Tamanna's mother is disappointed with her as she doesn't allow Tamanna to pursue her passion, preferring that she focus on her goal of becoming a doctor. This is exactly her parents' desire, not hers. She has always desired to pursue her passion and become a well-known fashion designer.

*"What the heck, instead of wasting your precious time on some meaningless drawings, you should be preparing for your final board exam? Gather them up and put them in the trash container before your father sees them. Stability is the key to life. Dreams belong to idiots and poets. You won't be fed by fashion."*Her mother becomes upset when she creates those priceless artworks at the early age of fifteen.

She started to collect things up, but regrettably, and unfortunately, her father was standing at the door of her room, observing everything. He then picked up a drawing and split the paper in two, and her father, Mr. Rakesh Gupta, confirmed this. *"This is your final opportunity. As a parent, I expect you to get a better grade than I did in my 12th grade when I received a 98%. But considering what I'm seeing, you're wasting your precious time on useless pursuits. I believe it will be challenging for you to receive a 60%. Now that you're prepared, allow me to make one more clarification: if you are unsure that you will be able to get 90%, you should at the very least be prepared to check into the hostel today."*

Her father screams at her mother as he leaves the room. *"Bharti, hurry and get me breakfast. Stop wasting time on her. I need to visit the hospital shortly."* Her mother frowned and walked away, leaving her alone in that room with those haphazard designs all over the floor. After gathering all of those patterns, she throws them in the trash and uses the bathroom. Dreams floated through Tamanna's heart like imprisoned birds under the shower.

Tamanna's heart, however, beat with a peculiar rhythm. She'd take breaks between stethoscope and injections to sketch. Her worn-out notebooks had silhouettes of flowing dresses, elaborate needlework, and daring necklines. The colors streamed from her soul: azure blues, sunny oranges, and midnight black. Fashion was her sanctuary, a place where her mind could weave threads into beautiful tapestries.

Tamanna's nights were her refuge. Under the moon's silver gaze, she'd trace imaginary hemlines on her quilt. Her fingers yearned for fabrics—the coolness of silk, the weight of velvet. She'd imagine herself backstage at fashion shows, adjusting collars and straightening lapels. But when dawn broke, she'd fold her dreams neatly, tucking them away like precious saris in an old trunk.

We pretend to be experts all the time, yet life still surprises us and has a plan for us. Tamanna has a similar experience. She used to dream of being a successful designer with a job in the industry and a plethora of awards, medals, and trophies. But at the next moment, she was just a shy little child who had been humiliated by her parents.

She was taking a bath feeling broken up by her parents' reaction to her wanting to be a fashion designer instead of a doctor. Just as she was standing beneath the shower, the voice came with the laughter of Sharon her neighbor and only close friend *"Hello! Tammy, may I come in? I'm eager to help if needed, and I have no trouble entering because you have not closed the door."*

Since they were young, Sharon has been her neighbor and a close friend. She also constantly encouraged her, praising her designs and motivating her to work towards her passion. She was the one who kept her ideas hidden from everyone, especially her parents.

She once brought all of her drawings to an institute when she was twelve, but unfortunately, the owner of the institute knew Sharon's parents and told everything to her father later in the evening when they both met in the clubhouse.

"Hello! David" the owner of the institute Mr. Shubhankar greets him

"Hello! Shubhankar, how are you?" Mr. David replied

*"I am good buddy; your daughter came to the institute today along with a complete sketchbook of fabulous and way beyond gorgeous designs,"*Shubankar said this and made a gesture to appreciate her work.

"What designs, she never told me anything about it," David asks in shock.

"No, she did not draw; those designs are made by her friend Tamanna, as she told me," Shubhankar replied.

*"Okay"*Before David understands the situation Shubhankar asks *"I am running late, I need to go home early today"* and leaves him with so many unanswered questions.

Fortunately, her parents are not like Tamanna's parents, thus everything turned out for the best in the end for

Sharon. That day, Tamanna and Sharon were brought into the living room by her father, and he asked, "*Among you who made these designs?*" as he showed them the designs that he collected from Shubhankar before he left for his home. Knowing that Sharon wasn't interested in drawing, her father asked again when she initially raised her hand. "*So please, without hiding who it is, just tell me who made these beautiful designs?*" With apology, Sharon looks at Tamanna, and it seems to both of them that he is going to tell Tamanna's father. So they both jumped up in front of her dad and started crying and begged him not to tell Tamanna's dad about this.

Sharon's father, Mr. David, embraced them warmly and remarked, "*You haven't done anything wrong, and so you don't need to be worried. The owner of the institute went crazy over them and said, "I haven't seen such designs," as they are so beautiful.*"Together, they took a deep breath, and Sharon said, "*Precisely, I always appreciate them but her parents won't allow her ever.*" Tamanna agreed and lowered her head down as if someone had placed a heavy plate on her head.

Mr. David stated,"*Today's kids have to deal with a harsh truth: parents don't respect their freedom and passion; instead, they want their kids to follow the path they want. Sharon, I've never inquired about your ideal work. Do you have any plans for your future or the type of career you wish to pursue, similar to Tamanna's? You may inform me, and I promise not to interfere with your decision and to even set up your career properly.*"

Without hesitating, Sharon said,"*Papa, I want to be a model.*" "*Model!!*" Mr. David was shocked but then realized that she should follow her dream of being a model since she had decided at age twelve. He accepted without more inquiry, Sharon hugged her father and said,"*You are the best father in the world."*

When Tamanna saw them, she stood very still and spoke the words, *"I wish you were my father."* Returning her hug, Mr. David continued, *"I am like your father; whenever you feel that you need me, do not hesitate to come and ask for help. I will always be there for you"* After nodding and considering what occurred in Sharon's house, Tamanna went home. She secretly kept thinking if telling her parents that she had always wanted to become a fashion designer would be a great idea then after a while she said to herself *"No"*.

She used to pray and express her dreams in hopes that one day they might come true at a very ancient temple she must pass on her way home. She didn't say anything about her pain to anyone except the idol of Vishnu Ji at this temple.

From her rooftop, she would observe the stars and wonder whether they whispered secrets to other dreamers. The banyan tree listened, letting its roots take in her unsaid wants. Tamanna's drawings were kept out of sight, buried within biology and chemistry textbooks. Her parents, who had no idea that their daughter's soul was bound with invisible glittering crystals, and they keep, complimented her pragmatic approach.

The Temple of Disguised Echoes is located in the center of Ajmer, where the passage of time has created its historic tapestry. Its walls are weighed down by thousands of years, and its towers reach high into the sky. Nisang Ji, a mysterious character dressed in saffron robes, is accommodated within these holy walls. Nisang Ji's appearance is a patchwork of youth and wisdom. His youthful, untainted cheekbones arc like crescent moons. Oh, that smile of his! It's like a ray of sunshine peeking through the clouds during rain. The pilgrims' burdens are erased as it warms their hearts. His hair falls down his back like silvery moonlight. Earmarked with jasmine flowers, it projects a scent of devoted love.

Nisang Ji challenges the year's calendar at eighty. His skin, torched red by the desert sun, is still unforgiving, like parchment marked with stories of devotion. The stones of the temple whisper secrets into his eyes, which are twin pools of obsidian. The devout see eternity reflected to them in his eyes, a timeless mirror.

The real wonder of the temple is his eyes—deep, bottomless pools of light within them are the universe itself. He bestows blessings upon children, and they shine like far stars. Solace is sought by pilgrims in such eyes. They see glimpses of the dance of the gods, cosmic cycles, and former incarnations. With a steady look, Nisang Ji listens as though interpreting the heavenly message inscribed in their minds.

His robes of saffron envelop him in shades of the time of sunset. A tale is revealed by each fold, such as the arrival of a holy calf, the first monsoon following an extended drought, or the echo of a long-forgotten chant. As he goes, his movements as river stones and mala beads click quietly. An old artifact, an amulet, hangs around his neck. With a heartbeat that connects worlds, its ruby core beats with vitality. The origin of Nisang Ji is rarely discussed, although pilgrims insist that it contains the mysteries of the temple. Nisang Ji defies his years with his graceful movements. His footsteps mimic the pulse of devotion that breaths through the temple.

He holds firm hands, gently urging ancient logs to blaze as he maintains the holy fire. Gardens resound with the richness of his laughter, reminiscent of temple bells. Little ones sit at his feet, wide-eyed, drawn by it. The flowering lotus growing in the mud represents life; he reminds them "Absorb them both."

The agelessness of Nisang Ji is not an illusion; its dedication became crystal clear. He takes a dip in the holy water of the *temple, his skin kissed by the moonlight. He invokes the heat of the sun by chanting mantras at sunrise. And when the stars come together, he looks up, searching the constellations for answers. The priest who transcends time, Nisang Ji, whispers, "Every breath contains the divine. Within, remain timeless."So Nisang Ji stands a link between worlds, a keeper of whispers, and the everlasting allure of Ajmer.*

There are folders of blank pages throughout his room and nobody is allowed in. Since he had grown up in the temple, his guru had permitted him to pick up that blank paper from Terries every day at 7:00 p.m. As a result, he finally gained the authority to collect them. Over time, the subsequent disciples had come to assume this duty. Take it out of the Terries, knot it in a folder, and close it.

Tamanna used to visit the old banyan tree at that ancient temple, which served as her covert hideout. Its leaves murmured stories long forgotten and its roots wrapped themselves around the soil like an affectionate pair of arms. Tamanna used to sit there and fantasize while supporting her sketchbook on her knees. She saw spotlights, clapping, runways—the world outside the old walls of Ajmer. Every time, Nisang ji would express her gratitude, offer her a lollipop, and assure her that one day she would realize her aspirations. When she hears such words, her face brightens, but she quickly gets disappointed when she sees her parents' faces.

That day, Tamanna visited the temple on her way home from Sharon's residence and questioned to Nisang ji, *"Sharon's father is the best, but my father doesn't understand my passion for designing, he thinks that becoming a doctor is the only option to be a successful person. You always tell me that I will fulfill my dreams at some point, but I don't feel like that, since my parents won't let me pursue my dream of being a fashion designer. I'm not interested in becoming a doctor."*

"Everyone has a reason for being here on Earth, and they must fulfill their karma," Nisang ji said with a smile. *"You are being guided towards success by your karma; believe me, it is written and you will finally obtain it. Just be cheerful and leave it on time. Lord Vishnu will help you in a little while."*

Having nowhere else to go, she sets out towards her home, a place she seldom visits with delight. She is not permitted to eat, play, smile, or even breathe at home. There is nothing she can do by choice she has to follow her parent's decisions only. Her dreams are slowly vanishing into a very shallow sea, and she can't bring herself to confront her parents.

She created a lovely artwork for Nisang Ji when she came home that evening, and she gave it to him before she left for school the next morning. *"This is how your dhoti kurta should be worn; it will suit you well. This was created by me just for you."* Tamanna said this and then gave the artwork to Nisang Ji. *"I will definitely try this on a special occasion,"*Nisang ji said, passing her a lollipop. From that point on, Tamanna would make a stop at the temple on her way home from school every day.

There, she would spend some time talking about her emotions while standing in front of Vishnu Ji's idol. Therefore, today also she was, feeling bad about what had occurred this morning; she decided to make one trip to that temple before heading back home today. When she first arrived at the temple, she realized something wasn't as usual there was a strange presence she felt that day. Anyways, She leaned down and bowed down in front of the statue of Vishnu ji, and she couldn't find Nisang ji, she began mumming *"My father will never understand my feelings what should I do, but it's the worst day of my life and I believe I won't be able to achieve 90%, Papa will definitely send me to the hostel today"*

"Do not be afraid, my child," a voice murmured as she was entirely immersed in praying. *"The right time is here, and everything will be well."*Nisang Ji, speaking from behind, recreated the outfit she had sketched for him almost three years back when she was twelve years old. Tamanna bowed in front of Nisang ji, saying, *"Finally, you wore this dhoti kurta that I designed for you."* *"How do you know that I am frightened right now, and by the way, what were you saying?"*He just handed Tamanna the lollipop as usual in answer to her query, saying,*"Don't worry, this is the right time."*When she was ready to leave the temple with the blessings, Nisang Ji gave her a strange look and said,*"Just remember one thing: your courage will make you something, and things will happen for your good; just do not be afraid to follow your dreams, or you will lose everything."*

When she arrived home, she was still thinking about what Nisang ji had told her. However, she eventually lost the will to push the bell, but she had no other choice, so she pressed the bell button, and her mother answered the door. She asked her first *"how the examination went,"* to which she replied, *"Very nice,"* before entering the home. Her father was seated on the couch, which she had never seen because he worked long hours and rarely came home in the middle of the day. She seemed surprised, but she masked it by strolling quietly to her room. However, before she arrived, her father used a harsh and ridiculing tone. *"This theory of fear always works, so I know you will score 90%."* She whirled back as soon as he said this, adding, *"Yes, papa, it works,"* and rushed into her room.

She didn't open the door to her room until her mother knocked for dinner. *"Open the gate, Tamanna; it is 8 p.m. and dinner is served,"* her mother remarked. She unlocked the gate and told her mother, *"I'm not feeling well and a little drained, so please get my dinner in the room only."* Her mother refused at first but later accepted because her father was on tour. *"Okay, but why you are still wearing your uniform, change your uniform first."* Her mother said and gave her the meal she ate and went to bed early that day. It was just 9 p.m., and she slept thinking about what Nisang ji said to her.

Perhaps destiny had a bolt of silk waiting for her, a bolt that would break her quiet. Perhaps the banyan tree, ancient and wise, would speak bravery through her veins. Tamanna embroidered her dreams in invisible thread for the time being, hoping that one day, her runway would spread beyond Ajmer's horizon, and her name would shine like a sequin in the sun.

II
Chapter two

Tamanna heard her mother say, ***"Wake up, you won't be able to reach for your exam on time,"*** in an unclear voice. She awoke quickly, went to the bathroom, and shut the door. Everything in the room has changed, including the small-sized books of 12th standard are now changed into heavy medical volumes on the shelf next to her study table. It is now a dark room with new dark shades of curtains so that the sun's rays cannot enter. She hurriedly dressed for college after using the bathroom. As a result, it seems that Tamanna Gupta balanced obedience and passion.

She concealed her sketchbook in her backpack while attending college in cotton suits. Through lectures reverberated through the corridors, her thoughts strayed to bias cuts and uneven high-efficiency medical systems. When she would go by the tailor's store and get a sight of the cloth-draped mannequins, her heart would race like an insect attached to a far-off flame. She became upset for a time after seeing an extra copy of her design that she had given to Nisang ji while getting dressed, but once more her mother's voice prompted her to put her dream aside and concentrate on her final test of her final year of medical school. ***"Coming Mommy, I'm ready,"*** she said as she hurriedly gathered all the exam-related items she would need and exited the room.

When she was returning home from her exam, she heard Sharon, a prominent model who currently resides in Mumbai, calling her ***"Tammy."*** She approached Tamanna with a cigarette in her hand while wearing stylish modern attire. ***"Hey! How are you doing, Tammy? You still look like Aunty."*** As usual, Sharon teased her by saying this. ***"Aunty is fine, but you say rapchik chick, how come you look so amazing, and when did you start smoking? Bad habit"*** Tamanna answered.

"Look, I am in Ajmer for two or three days only and want to spend as much time as I can with you these days so no arguments you are coming with us right now," Sharon replied, tossing away the cigarette. Tamanna wanted to go, but she said, ***"I can't right now, but we will meet in the evening preferably when you are free,"*** due to her parent's restrictions. Sharon started dragging her but Tamanna objected, saying, ***"You know mumma will not allow me to go, please understand,"*** but Sharon did not want to hear it and continued to drag Tamanna along with her while holding her hand. Sharon glances back and responds, ***"Shut up, I'm coming wait,"*** to her companions' continued yell, ***"Sharon, please come fast, we are getting late."*** ***"You please go and enjoy with your friends; I will meet you in the evening,"*** Tamanna stated. ***"Okay, you are staying with me tonight and I will call you before I leave Pushkar,"*** Sharon stated as she and her companions went for tracking on the dunes of Pushkar.

As Tamanna began to proceed forward, she heard Nisang ji say, ***"Please stay, we need to talk come,"*** as she approached the old temple and bowed her head from the outside. She felt embarrassed and avoided talking to Nisang ji after when he had informed her that day that *"it is you who needs to gather courage and fight for your dreams else you won't be able to achieve your dreams."* She looked back and wanted to chat, but she lacked the guts to do so. She rushed and made it home, but as she stood at the door, all she could think was that she ought to share her dream with her parents once. She rings the bell and begins gathering the guts to say *"I want to be a fashion designer"*, but her mother asks, *"How was the exam?"* as soon as the door opens before she can say anything. *"What percentage do you anticipate?"* She entered the room with her mouth hanging out and said, *"Above 90."*

Expectations are usually painful and may occasionally shatter someone to the point where they lose all motivation to live. We always wait for the angels, and they arrive as well, but unless we have the confidence to put ourselves out there, not even the angels can act. Tamanna experienced a similar situation. She had aspirations of being a fashion designer but lacked the bravery to pursue them.

Tamanna was once told by Nisang ji, *"I pray for the day when you can manage your fear. Just once, with all of your courage, tell your parents what you want. Only then will your dream come true, and only then will angels assist you."* God writes each person's destiny individually and gives us the courage to fulfill it, so this may be our final chance. However, humans must recognize this opportunity and make the correct choice at the appropriate moment. However, we just need to always be prepared for that final opportunity since we never know when or which one may present itself in our lives. Our lives are greatly impacted by religion since it is the only thing that gives us the strength needed to face and overcome any challenge. Until something extraordinary occurs to us, either good or tragic, we do not value trust.

Sharon was on one side, having the support of her parents, which enabled her to find the strength to pursue her ambition. Tamanna, on the other hand, had dreams but in secret as she is worried about her parents since they never gave a damn about them and constantly tried to force their will on her. It's not that she didn't try, but once trust is shattered, it's hard to predict when it will heal.

The phone rang *"tring tring,"* and Tamanna's mother answered it loudly, calling Tamanna, who was by herself and idly sitting in her room. *"Tamanna, this is Sharon's call,"* she said, setting the receiver down on the landline's table before returning to her work in the kitchen. Sharon did not say hello or engage in any formal discussion; instead, she just said, *"Wear sexy clothes and come to my house immediately.""Hey, I don't know anyone there; hasn't even asked mummy yet, and now all of a sudden, mummy won't let me come."* She begins to make meaningless explanations, but Sharon has known her since she was a little girl, so she ends the conversation, and Tamanna returns to her room.

The doorbell rang at the moment she walked into the room. Tamanna was requested to open the gate by her mother, as she was busy in the kitchen. *"Where is your mum?"* Sharon said as Tamanna opened the gate. Sharon approached swiftly in the kitchen, asking, *"Aunty, I am going back to Mumbai the day after tomorrow so I am taking Tammy with me tonight, I want to spend the night with my one and only childhood friend."* Tamanna stayed standing at a distance.

After saying *"Okay,"* Tamanna's mother resumed slicing the veggies. Sharon takes Tamanna's hand and leads her into her room. She opens her closet and begins looking for something special. A minute later, she finds Tamanna's school outfit. She grabs it and leads Tamanna back inside. She had a really angry expression on her face, but it went beyond simple anger to a sort of expression that normally appears when something or someone genuinely desires something and ruins it. Tamanna simply took her hand in silence before leaving for her home.

"I should have done it years ago so that today you might doing what you have always dreamt, now stay quiet and just walk with me we are going to spend a night which you will never forget and hope so you might get some courage to be a rebel." Sharon continued walking while holding Tamanna's hand. *"But I did not say a word yet,"* Tamanna said, looking at Sharon before they both burst out laughing.

"This is precisely the issue you face; you never express it." This was uttered by Sharon in a very mocking tone. As soon as they enter the room, everyone yells out loud, *"Surprise,"* and they both arrive at Sharon's house, where everyone else is waiting to surprise Tamanna. *"You planned everything for me, Sharon. You are such a great friend. I missed you so much,"* Tamanna said, shockingly throwing her arms around Sharon. After saying this, Tamanna began slapping Sharon's shoulder softly. She gave her a strong, tender hug and remarked, *"Missed you too. Everyone is eager to see you, so don't spend any more time."*

"This is Divya, she is also a model and my senior in the industry, Divya's face is a canvas brushed by angels," Sharon said as she introduced each person in the room to Tamnna one by one. Her almond-shaped eyes, the color of the twilight sky, are framed by high cheekbones. Her lips curves like the crescent moon when she smiles, evoking adoration.

"This is Pulkit; he is my senior and the face of numerous print advertising agencies." Although most male models are over six feet tall, Pulkit is a petite 5'8" powerhouse in the fashion industry. Pulkit's visage is a symmetry study. His cheeky smile is framed by a jawline as sharp as a tailor's scissors. His eyes are secretive pools of mystery that the camera can only peek into.

"This is Shashwat, my boyfriend and a ramp model just like me." Shashwat goes down the catwalks with confidence, even if he is not very tall. He's become a sought-after male model because of his chiseled looks and captivating charisma. However, underneath the camera's lights is a deep-seated ambition to enter the acting profession and leave the glare of the runway.

Before Tamanna could say hello to anyone, they all yelled, ***"You are Tamanna and you are Sharon's best friend, and you want to be a fashion designer."*** A broad smile emerged on her face.

Tamanna was led to the kitchen by Sharon, who wrapped her hand over Tamanna's neck. ***"Let's begin the night we will all remember, so you guys set up the things here, and Tamanna and I will grab some snacks for you guys,"*** they said before heading off. ***"Tammy, I understand that you missed me and that you followed your parents' instructions. Aside from that, what else have you done that I should know about?"*** Sharon asked Tamanna. Tamanna started pouring coke into the glasses and said, ***"Nothing much, this is my life, Sharon, I can't do anything else, and I can never go beyond that so I am very sorry to disappoint you but I do not have any spicy story for you yet." "Hey!" "Those glasses aren't meant for coke,"*** Tamanna interrupted. ***"Oh my! "I apologize, I didn't know,"*** Tamanna apologizes. ***"Grab the glasses and come on over. We're going to cook a spicy story tonight so*** *you might have something to say when we get together next time."* And they both entered the living room, where the couch was occupied by everyone else.

*"Tamanna, we've heard a lot about you and your designs more than anything else, so it seems like Sharon talks about you and your designs all the time,"*Divya said. *"I truly do appreciate them, and I apologize, but I utilized some of them for personal use without your consent since they were so lovely. However, Sharon told me I could use them when I asked."*

"Not only you, I have used most of them many times, and you know one interesting fact she designed my school uniform once when we were in school," Sharon interrupted Divya in the middle of her statement.

Sharon got up, retrieved Tamanna's uniform which she bought from her house, gave it to Tamanna, and told her to wear it the way you had made it for me at school. Tamanna got nervous and said, *"No way, I'm not wearing this; I'll do something nice with your dress instead."* However, she said, *"I'm not asking you; I want you to wear this and be a part of our team. Come on, hurry up; we're all waiting."* Sharon leads Tamanna inside the room while holding her hand. When they finally emerged, after about 10 minutes, everyone was in astonishment. Tamanna looked as stunning and seductive as a supermodel, and people couldn't stop staring at her. She appeared as though she had come directly down from heaven.

On the other hand, she just stood there, a bit uncomfortable and bashful. Tamanna had never experienced such joy; to her, this occasion was like receiving a medal. She had a fresh vigor that she had not experienced before. It makes her as happy as she had never heard such words from anyone except Sharon rather she always heard words from her parents which killed the dream and ruined her self-respect until today. At that moment, Tamanna felt a new type of faith and energy strike her like lightning, and she let out a loud *"I love you, Sharon."* Once she had yelled loud enough for the first time, after a while, she realized and hugged Sharon for a bit and the entire space was filled with an awkward silence.

*"The weather is youthful; we are youthful too, why not go for a night out for this fresh version of Tamanna today?"*Pulkit replied, breaking the ice. *"This sounds fantastic, let's check out Ajmer's night-time beauty,"* Divya added. *"Okay, but the problem is that we have never seen night life of Ajmer, because I left Ajmer at an early age just after my 12th grade, and you all know Tamanna very well, she hasn't seen day life properly,"* Sharon stated after exchanging a look with Tamanna.

They all decided to watch a movie in a theatre even though Shashwat, one of them, had started looking up information on Ajmer's nightlife as they were talking about it. Even after giving Sharon a lot of reasons to change Tamanna's no into a yes, they all headed to the movie theatre. Tamanna is still not fond of going out, but Sharon and her friends converted her no into yes, and finally she said yes.

It was a strange night, today Tamanna, who had been buried for a long time, was given wings. However, it is argued that obtaining anything requires a great deal of effort, making it harder to determine its worth. Tamanna too had the same situation today.

For some reason, she continued having the impression that she would wake up from her sleep soon and this reality would stay a dream, even if she didn't want to accept that everything that was happening to her was true. Everyone can dream, but Tamanna quit because she was afraid of her parents' reactions.

In any case, when everyone was prepared to go, they all sat in the car, but as Pulkit was the superior driver, he chose to take the wheel. It was going well as Sharon and Tamanna were traveling there, sitting in the rear seat and holding hands, but something odd happened when Sharon said to Tamanna, *"Hey! When you were at home, Tammy, you were not wearing those earrings.""I don't remember about earrings,"*Tamana said, resting her head on Sharon's shoulder and expressing gratitude for the lovely day.

After taking a long pause *"You know, Tammy, I've always hoped that you'll stand up for your dream and fight for it, but you never have. Why is that?"* Sharon questioned Tamanna.

Tamanna inhaled deeply and murmured,

"Everyone has a unique destiny, and regardless of what we desire or don't want, we only receive what is predetermined for us. Not that I haven't attempted anything at all. However, as trust starts to erode, we lose our ability to distinguish between right and wrong. I purposefully put the designs on the study table the day before our 12th-grade exams so that my mother would see them and perhaps realize what I wanted to accomplish and become. I wanted her to think highly of me, I wanted her respect for my passion but that didn't happen. In actuality, the reverse of what I had imagined occurred. Dad went on to say was the murder of my dreams and my beliefs." Sharon had nothing to say after hearing Tamanna's words, so she sat silently with her head on the vehicle window, waiting for the cinema hall to arrive.

Finally, they arrived, and everyone felt a little awkward as it was a strange area, so no one was interested in going, but Pulkit and Shashwat persuaded everyone to come and see the movie on the condition that if anything in there seemed odd, we would leave right away. So, everyone entered the cinema hall; it was empty, and no one was at the ticket window, so everyone moved right in, and the movie was ready to begin. Except for Tamanna, everyone else wanted to smoke, so they all went outside and left Tamanna inside.

After a few minutes, Tamanna heard a strange voice mention her name *"Tamanna"*. She first avoided that voice, but it returned, *"Tamanna"* This time it was much heavier than before and she began fleeing out of the cinema theatre, only to find Sharon. On the steps, she met Sharon, she hugged her saying, ***"Please never do this kind of joke again"*** Sharon didn't grasp it, so she remarked, ***"What joke, I didn't do anything,"*** and held her hand before returning to watch the movie. While seated, she saw Tamanna's earrings had altered and were not the same as before. ***"Now I wanted to know that how are you changing your earrings again and again?"*** Sharon inquired and touched the earrings with a weird expression. Tamanna said, ***"I have no clue what you are saying, hey it is starting"*** as the movie began, and everyone else joined them.

They all had fun enjoying the movie, and during the intermission, they all went for a smoke, but Tamanna chose to stay because she did not smoke. When they all departed, Tamanna heard that same unusual voice again and assumed it was someone among them playing a trick on her, so she didn't notice, but she gradually became hypnotized by that sound and stood up and walked out another door. And entered a dark area where everyone was dressed in a black outfit. Tamanna is suddenly in front of a crystal ball that slowly emerges from the circle's center. The head of the strangely dressed individuals executes a small sound, and Tamanna returns to normal. The head told her that no one would hear her call for assistance when she saw them, adding that there was a reason why she was there and how long she wanted to remain would be up to her. Tamanna said, ***"Who are you, and where am I?"*** to this weird person.

In the shadowed depths of a forgotten mansion, Ezra emerges—a phantom draped in obsidian, a voiceover says as he breaks out into laughter. The whisper of tenebrous cloth and the slight rustling of silk announce his arrival. His face is hidden behind a mask as dark as the abyss, a relic from another time, its surface inscribed with mysterious markings. All except his eyes are obscured by the mask, which fits his face like a second skin and sparkles with unearthly wisdom.

His attire, a grotesque symphony of textures, is beyond the comprehension of mortals. He is surrounded by dark velvet clothing, the bottom edge of which scrapes the chilly, uneven floor. Every stride he makes reverberates like a lament through the barren hallways. The borders of the robe shred as though they have been touched by deterioration itself, and its collar rises high, framing his shrouded features.

Underneath the cloak, Ezra is dressed in an antiquated, timeless suit. The material clings to his muscular physique, drawing attention to how thin his appearance is. The buttons are made of bone that has been fashioned from the remains of long-dead souls. His fingerless, ink-stained gloves bring up thoughts of the magical ceremonies and forbidden books.

However, the mask is what attracts everyone who sees him in wonder. Its surface is asymmetrical, twisted, and twisted as though sculpted by insanity. There are gaping eye holes that are empty of pupils and sharp slits that function as nostrils. The mouth opens out like a fissure, exposing teeth that are sharpened to a point. When Ezra speaks, his voice is like a ghostly whisper, sending shivers down everyone's spine.

His motivation is still a mystery. Some claim he is a guardian against the invasion of ordinary reality, a guardian of secrets lost. Some say that he is a ghost that appears when the curtain between realms gets thin, a sign of an approaching catastrophe. They say that he can control invisible regions by channeling the powers of long-forgotten gods via his mask.

There is no emotion or trace of humanity in Ezra's eyes. With surgical precision, they slice through the darkness, dissecting souls. He walks as a ghost negotiating the edge between life and death, with purposeful elegance. His footprints are undetectable, and those who come into contact with him experience memory loss and a sense of sanity that slips through their fingers like sand.

So Ezra walks around, a living sentinel in black with his mask linked to his body. Although mortals can't understand his purpose, one thing is certain: to see his disguised face is to see the abyss itself—a revelation that, depending on a person's nature, might either drive them insane or enlighten them.

After hearing everything, and seeing Ezra, Tamanna fainted out, and an odd darkness descended upon the room.

III

Chapter three

Lakshya was a little child who lived in a peaceful area of Ajmer and had eyes that could hold galaxies. But his heart pounded to the beat of silver filigree and jewels. In the shadow of the dusty streets, Lakshya was quietly admiring the elaborate jewellery the women in his neighborhood wore, while other boys played cricket.

Born into a world of clashing wants, Lakshya Verma was a young man with ink-black hair and eyes that retained the glitter of unpolished jewels. Though his parents had mapped out a different route for him, one filled with engineering schematics and mathematical formulas, his heartbeat to the beat of creation. Lakshya's parents, Mr. and Mrs. Verma, were well-known engineers in the cobblestone lanes of Ajmer, where tradition lingered. Theirs was a legacy of consistency, reason, and foresight. They imagined their son engineering bridges and figuring out load-bearing capabilities, just like them. However, Lakshya's dreams were made from silver and silk threads.

Lakshya, a potential jewellery designer, found inspiration in the most unexpected places. His textbooks became his canvas, and the margins were adorned with intricate sketches of gem-encrusted necklaces, delicate bracelets, and ornate earrings. Algebraic equations transformed into flowing pleats, each fold representing the curvature of a gemstone. Geometry, once abstract lines on paper, now dictated the contours of his jewellery designs.

Mrs. Verma, his mother, had a saree collection that matched the colours of a peacock's feathers. Lakshya sneaked into her wardrobe one day as the sun sent golden rays across the space. As he unfolded a crimson silk saree, his fingers shook, whispering secrets of beauty and elegance. He wrapped the pallu around his lean shoulders, letting it flow like a cascade. Instead of a youngster, he saw a jewelled royal in the mirror. Dreams were woven into his flesh by the saree's threads as it clung to him. Lakshya whirled, seeing himself creating exquisite nose pins, anklets, and necklaces.

The weight of brocade and the softness of chiffon fascinated him. Lakshya's fingers ached to touch these fabrics, envisioning how they could be woven into exquisite pieces. He would sneak into his mother's wardrobe, draping her silk saris over his shoulders. In those stolen moments, he became a magician with thread and needle, stitching together dreams of opulence and elegance.

Lakshya's passion for jewellery design grew, and soon he was experimenting with metals, gemstones, and intricate settings. His creations told stories—of love, heritage, and the beauty that lay hidden in everyday life. As he honed his craft, he discovered that jewellery wasn't just an accessory; it was a reflection of the wearer's soul.

Nonetheless, the Verma home reverberated with parental expectations at the dinner table each evening. His father would firmly straighten his glasses and remark,

"Lakshya, your intelligence is astounding. Like me, engineering will be your area of focus. It's a stable job that offers security in an environment of uncertainty." Your future lies in engineering. His mother, as constant, would nod her head every time.

But Lakshya's dreams danced in different directions. He used to sneak out to the rooftop and look at the constellations when the moon was low. He uttered his hidden dream to the stars: to become a jewellery designer. Not just any designer, but one who created objects that murmured lost tales of love and tragedy, the type that adorned queens and courtesans.

His dreams were full of images of diamonds, the emotions concealed in their facets. Rubies flashed with fire, sapphires held the depth of midnight sky, and diamonds shone like unshed tears. Lakshya saw rings that joined souls over ages, bracelets that spoke secrets to wrists, and necklaces that ringed throats like pledges.

The Verma family, however, was uncompromising. *"Creating art is a pastime,"* his dad remarked. *"Engineering is a career."* They sent him to the renowned Institute of Technology when he was in 10th standard, where mathematics and slide rules took the place of sketchbooks and silenced his mind's creative symphony.

Lakshya suffered a broken heart. He went to thermodynamics courses, but designs of chandelier earrings filled his notebooks. He did exceptionally well on fluid dynamics examinations, but enamelling and lace work were his passions. Rather than using harsh language, his parents' cruelty was their inability to acknowledge him as an artist imprisoned in an engineer's cage.

Lakshya Verma had to balance between obedience and disobedience as a result. His heart begged for the jeweller's bench, but his mind forced him to take the path that directly led him to an engineering degree. His quiet companion, the moon, saw his tears as he worked behind closed doors to polish diamonds into tiny constellations.

Lakshya requested her mother to stay at home so that he could get some rest because he was exhausted from finishing his final test for the 12th grade today and his parents were gone at a marriage ceremony. Lakshya was encouraged to sketch some ideas while he was by himself. He chose a red silk sari from her mother's closet, draped it, and began to sketch a pair of lovely earrings and a necklace, but he slept on the couch just before he could finish the designs. Lakshya became engrossed in his work. Droplets of sapphire were cradled by silver wires that bent like vines. Whispers of woodlands and monsoons were uttered by emeralds. His fingers fluttered, his desire absorbed into the cushion. Lakshya drifted off to sleep as dusk painted the room. He closed his eyes and drifted on a sea of precious stones. Dreams of an opal-studded sky, a bracelet made from moonbeams, and a necklace of wishes whirled all about him.

His parents were upset to find him dressed like this when they got home a few hours later. He received an extremely harsh warning from his parents today. What difference does it make, even if he has a somewhat feminine appearance? Stated differently, this culture educates us to grow as individuals and to persuade our minds to embrace the impending change. However, we are only able to accept as much as suits our needs and preferences, consequently we don't.

"Lakshya, what are you doing with yourself?" His mother began to shout and cry as she finally saw him dressed as a woman. Lakshya, dressed in his mother's silk saree, was standing quietly in front of the mirror when he heard his mother yelling, ***"Verma ji, come and see,"*** from the other side of the door.

Then he wondered whether they would try to accept him in that same appearance, but it was not going to happen. Without giving it any thought, his father simply pulled out his belt and began striking him as soon as he arrived and observed him in this state. Grabbing his hand, his father pulled him out of the home. Without seeking clarification or making any inquiries, his father simply followed his moral convictions.

His neighbor and close buddy Shravan had immediate knowledge of everything that was taking place at Lakshya's house. That's why Shravan ran to get him and brought him home in the same state. Thank God! Shravan's parents have different opinions from others and recognize that every individual has a fantasy world of their own. When Shravan's father arrived in, he gave him his turquoise pajamas and instructed him to go change them first. ***"Everyone learns to live with time. Over time, only the brave individual who is willing to battle for their aspirations will triumph."*** As he was handing kurta pajamas, his father spoke.

Lakshya picked up the dress and proceeded to change in the room. Shravan also called Kabir to his house, and Kabir joined them just before Lakshya left the room after he had changed his clothing and returned to the living area where everyone else was seated. Shravan knew that Lakshya wasn't good and that we needed to do something special as his friends. Shravan's father urged him to spend some time sitting by himself with him once he got out.

"Kabir, Shravan simply ask your mother if dinner is ready to be served by going inside. I'd want to speak with

Lakshya alone." He was left alone with his father when Shravan and Kabir nodded their heads. *"Since when are you performing this?"*He made Lakshya to speak up about his dreams. *"My parents never gave me the time of day and always had forced me to become an engineer, even though I always wanted to be a jewellery designer. I initially understood at the age of twelve that understanding clothing was an essential requirement for designing jewellery. I therefore made my first contact with Mom's brand-new silk saree. Since then, I've made a lot more designs."* Say it and begin to cry uncontrollably once more.

"Let me tell you a story. I always wanted to be a writer, but my father pressured me to become an engineer instead. Today, I'm a successful engineer, and I've never gone back to writing." Saying so, Shravan's father displayed the journal to him. It was a minimum of twenty-page diary. *"This diary is barely fifteen or twenty pages long. How many more of these diaries have you already written?"* Lakshya enquired. *"This is all I have been able to write till now,"* remarked Shravan's father, bowing his head. *"For this reason, I comprehend the burden that an individual bears when their aspirations don't come true."*

Lakshya was still in shock from what had transpired in his home, but before Shravan's father could say anything more, Shravan and Kabir entered the room and said, *"Let's get ready, we're going to watch a movie tonight."* Shravan then turned to his father and said, *"Papa, the food is served. You may proceed.""Are none of you eating?"*Shravan's dad questioned them. *"No, we're going to check out an abandoned movie theatre that's located in one of Pushkar's valleys."*Shravan's father holds Lakshya's hand statingwhen they all were ready to leave *"Those who can fight for themselves can win, but those who accept everything* *before the fight, even God cannot do anything for them, so fight and fight with courage."*

Lakshya sat in the dark movie theatre, shadows created on the flaking background by the flickering projector. The ancient upholstery and nostalgia filled the air. Shravan and Kabir were whispering eagerly next to him about the movie they had just seen, discussing the surprising finale, tension, and narrative twists. Lakshya was still in shock from the emotional rollercoaster that was the movie.

Shravan and Kabir rose, their mischievous eyes flashing, as the interval approached near. With a gentle poke, Shravan stated, *"We're going for a smoke. Are you coming?"* Lakshya halted.He didn't smoke, and he didn't find it appealing to stand outdoors in the cool Ajmer night.*"No,"* he answered.*"I'm going to stay here."*

The theatre looked to shift as his pals vanished out the door. The buzz of the projector faded into a far-off echo as the temperature dropped. Lakshya looked about, unsure if he was seeing things or not. That's when he heard it: a melancholic tune that sounded like wind chimes in an abandoned garden.

He was drawn to the rear of the hallway by the sound, hypnotized. He trailed behind it, walking past rows of vacant chairs until he came to a thick velvet curtain. He pulled it out of the way to uncover a secret entrance. Then the voice called out to him again, *"Lakshya"* louder now.

Lakshya moved into the shadows. There was a squeak beneath his feet as he went down a small stairway. When he reached the bottom, he was in a room with just one crystal ball for light. The chamber had an old-world feel to it, with weird symbols and tattered tapestries hanging on the walls.

And there, in the middle of it all Ezra appeared the obsidian-draped phantom. Ezra's mask obscured his face, revealing only his eyes, which were a source of wickedness that appeared to reach deep into his soul. Ezra's voice boomed through the room, *"You've come." "Young one, the crystal ball discloses mysteries. Be alert."*

The images swirled as Lakshya stared into the ball; they showed a hurried version of Tamanna's life. Her hopes, her sorrows, and her laughter—all condensed into little seconds. The heart raced in Lakshya. *"Why is this happening to me?"* Lakshya stumbled,*"Who are you?"* *"Ezra"*, he answered

His gaze was fixed on the Ezra. *"I am the custodian of lost legends,"* he answered. *"The tale of Tamanna is simply a single strand in the thread of life. You have found an alternative, Lakshya; a route that deviates from the norm. Will you solve the secrets that lie within?"* Lakshya paused, caught between terror and fascination. The surface of the crystal ball sparkled with potential as it indicated.

He inhaled deeply. *"Explain to me,"* he muttered.Thus, Lakshya saw a vision of fate in that dim chamber under the historic theatre—a tapestry tangled with strands of time, love, and sacrifice. The mysterious student's guardian, Ezra, stood by and watched as the student's fate fell apart in front of him.

Perhaps fate had other plans. Perhaps the stars aligned to place him in the path of a certain However, Lakshya remained a star in prison for the time being, waiting for the day to arrive when his dreams would shine through the rough stone like a diamond.

Now that Ezra was gone, Lakshya was by himself in that dim chamber. He was afraid and unable to see any way out at this point, making it impossible for him to understand anything. Now, he could only see what Ezra had informed him was flashing before his eyes.

He could hear a weird sound coming from all directions in his ears. It took him a long time to realize what was going on, but eventually, when he tried to focus and pay attention to those voices, he began to comprehend. ***"Papa!"*** he said in a low voice. Even though those noises were still unclear, he rose from there, attempted to move forward, put his hands on the ground, and stood up.

After moving on, he came to a cave that had an endless number of exits. And it was difficult to figure out how to escape. Exhausted, he sat there for some time and began to reflect. He was unable to concentrate since he could still hear those odd whispering noises. A spirit appeared out of nowhere and passed through one of those endless doors before he could make sense of anything.

There was a very small sign above each door, which he discovered when he saw the spirit entering that door. And he began to consider again, attempting to make sense of them and find a way out, after noticing the symbols painted on each door individually.

Before he could make up his mind, two spirits entered and exited two separate doorways. The spirits would enter via one of the doorways every two to three seconds. He was now beginning to worry since he was losing all clues as to how to escape that location. He began to move towards a route, a bit terrified and a little anxious, believing that whatever happened might not be worse than this. After walking a short way, he noticed that the trail was getting smaller, and he knew he had to go. He managed to get out by using the path that was getting smaller, but he was still mystified as to why this had occurred.

Abruptly, he recalled the words that Shravan's father had spoken to him as they were leaving the home. ***"Those who can fight for themselves will prevail; but, even God will***

be powerless to help those who give up before the fight even begins." He had now resolved that he would not concede defeat in light of what he had stated. He took a step forward and began to examine the signs displayed above each door closely.

Even after witnessing several of these indications one after the other, he was unable to comprehend much of them. The first sign said that a guy was falling from above; the second said that a youngster was going to school; the third showed a man soaring in the air; and the fourth said that a man was being pursued. It had taken him a long time to comprehend these signals. However, he has sadly not been able to figure out the secret of whether a door or sign is there and will enable him to escape. The objective, he thought, was to keep going ahead, but the area was so confusing that he had also forgotten where he had originally begun his journey.

He continued to walk while carrying his parents' thoughts constantly in mind. Somewhere along the line, he began to believe that maybe God had sent Ezra to rescue him from the spot where he was beginning to suffocate. In the meantime, a great number of spirits were arriving and going via various doors. He had barely gone through four doors up to this point when he heard sobs. **"Please help me,"** Tamanna begged as she sobbed while sitting in a rock's shadow.

IV
Chapter four

Lakshya exclaimed, *"Hey! Before coming here, I saw you as the same girl in the crystal ball."* Tamanna was simply sobbing and wailing while she sat there. *"Don't be scared; I'm trapped here too, and I won't hurt you,"* Lakshya says this and reaches out to touch Tamanna, hoping that she will trust him. However, Tamanna was unable to trust him at first, so she turned down his offer of assistance. Suddenly, however, she grabs his hand and draws him closer to her, sensing the approach of an evil spirit. *"Dear"*, Lakshya said, *"Hey! How are you spending your time?"* His perplexities grew over what had just happened and why she pulled his hand. *"I was just saving you there was an evil spirit"* Tamanna answered.

"Prasang informed me that he became trapped here with us, but he ultimately found his way. But first, he told me all he'd learned from someone who had been there before." Tamanna responded.

"So, tell me did he tell you how we can get out of here." Lakshya inquired with curiosity.

"Unfortunately, now we are stuck in the world of dreams, and we will remain stuck until we find a way to fulfill our

dreams." Tamanna turns around as she speaks, and her earring falls. Lakshya took up the earring and remarked, *"How."*

Tamanna noted that her earring fell and turned back to pick it up, but before she could, Lakshya grabbed it up and was astonished, asking Tamanna, *"Is this yours?"*

"Nah, suddenly this came to my ears, I don't know how," Tamanna remarked, taking her earring back from Lakshya.

"I made this" Lakshya said,

"Are you a designer?". Tamanna inquired.

"No," he replied.

"Then," she asked.

"I mean, yes, it is very complicated. I am still not able to understand what happened to me and the very next moment I saw this, it was very strange as I made a sketch of this design and I saw this in real, it is just so beautiful." He holds that earring and asks Tamanna if she liked it. *"This was the first design that I made for a western dress, otherwise I made designs only for Indian attire, and did you like it"*

She just stated, *"Yes, I liked them; they are so beautiful."*

When Lakshya told her all of this, she felt the same energy she did whenever she showed Sharon her new designs.

She gently touched his shoulder and whispered, *"I understand now. Let's get moving or we'll be stuck here forever."*

They both begin going forward and barely add two more steps.

Lakshya questioned Tamanna, *"What is the meaning of these signs above each door"*

Tamanna quickly responded: *"We are in the world of dreams and millions of people must be dreaming in this world right now and all these signs depict their dreams."*

"*Then why did we get stuck here if it is a world of dreams?*"he questioned Tamanna.

Tamanna reacted: "*We got stuck because we have never dared to fulfill our dream, we never allowed our dream to reach its destination, and we never found the courage to follow the path which our dreams have shown us so, we eventually lost in our dream*"

Lakshya inquired again. "*How do you know about it, since when you are here?*"

"*You want to know everything right now,*" Tamanna said, looking frustrated at him.

Following a moment's stroll, she responded "*I met three people till now since I stuck here, one was a 30-year-old man Mr. Jack, he wants to be a singer but his parents wanted him to join their family business and keep singing as his only hobby.*" Pause while speaking.

"*So, how did he manage to get out of here?*" Lakshya inquired.

Tamanna took a big breath and shook her head before saying, "*He couldn't get out of here and died.*"

Lakshya became worried after hearing about what happened to Jack. So he remained silent for more than a minute, as did Tamanna, but Tamanna broke the unpleasant quiet by telling another story about Bhaskar, an adolescent. "*Bhaskar, was a teenager and he wished to become a dancer, his father was against his dancing passion and so he decided to leave home to pursue the passion at a very early age but here in the dream world he was captured by some evil spirit and he suddenly disappeared.*"

Tamanna advised Lakshya,"*Stay away from any bad thoughts here because the bad spirits only attack those who abandon their passion and dreams and fall into bad company or alcoholism, smoking, etc.*" So stay away from such *companies; you may receive offers here individually."*

Lakshya nodded and said, *"What about the third?"*Tamanna responded, *"His name was Prasang and his passion was to become a photographer, but he never told his parents."*Lakshya followed Tamanna. After a minute, Lakshya inquired *"What happened to Prasang then"*. Tamanna stayed quiet and did not answer the question.

*"Have you tried going into any of the doors yet?"*Tamanna questioned him.

*"Yes one but the door started shrinking so I swiftly moved out and saved my life,"*Lakshya responded.

*"He didn't come out he went into the wrong door which is not made for him and so I do not know what happened to him after that,"*Tamanna stated this with a sorrowful heart because he was the only one there to support her.

After almost half an hour, Lakshya and Tamanna remained silent and continued to travel to find their way out. While strolling, they both see the signs and occasionally exchange looks of no before moving on. Tamanna and Lakshya were surrounded by symbols in their ethereal dream world. Each one shimmered with secret meaning, waiting to be discovered. Their common passion for artistic expression had led them here, free of their parents' expectations.

Tamanna observed a few indications and shared her thoughts with Lakshya, adding,*"Since we are in the world of dreams and every sign has meaning, what would happen if we read the signs differently since you enjoy creating and I enjoy designing as well? What therefore must be the meaning of the symbol we often see in our dreams? "*She points her finger up to the notice above the entrance that says vehicle accident. So, they both begin to simulate their imagination. Tamanna questioned Lakshya, *"What do you think about this? Who* *could dream of a car accident?"*

Lakshya said, *"I don't think anyone could ever dream of a car accident; these placards might represent people's anxiety. It may be a nightmare."*

*"But what does it signify, and how can we determine it? Because this is the only way to get out of here as I suppose."*Tamanna asked.

*"You were constantly afraid of your parents, and I am likewise afraid of my parents. So, if I evaluate my fantasies up to this day, I've always wanted to escape and go somewhere where no one would criticize me, where I could wear whatever I wanted and make whatever I wanted.*Lakshya responded.

"You're right. I always wanted to leave home because of my parent's pressure, but I was afraid to leave the house without their consent. So, for me, escape is the common link between us: we both want to leave our world. Let's look up anything relevant to escape." Tamanna informs Lakshya and starts walking towards the next door. While moving on, she was thinking of Nisang ji's last words to her about being courageous.

They both interpret the phoenix feather (A lighthouse-shaped column of flames that flickered.) they saw as a sign in their unique ways. It may also give you the confidence to confront some of life's most tough difficulties. Phoenixes in dreams symbolize rebirth, metamorphosis, eternity, immortality, and resurrection. Because the phoenix must die to rise, it may also represent a fear of death. Tamanna's heartbeat as she recognized that the phoenix represented persistence and rebirth. *"Maybe this feather holds the courage to rise from our ashes,"* she said Lakshya.

Lakshya concurred, and without much discussion, they both concluded that it was not the door they were looking for, so they proceeded to the next door. The distance between the doors is nearly a mile; therefore they should keep chatting to keep themselves motivated, since stopping may discourage them.

Tamanna initiated the conversation by asking Lakshya, *"Have you ever had the feeling that you should commit suicide rather than live such a life?"* Lakshya responded, *"Never, since I wanted to live, pursue my passion, and become a great designer. It is not my fault that I am a bit feminine; in fact, I believe it is a gift from God, thus I never had this emotion. However, because of my parents' constraints, I have never stood up to them, which may be my greatest fear."*

Lakshya then asked Tamanna the same question: *"Have you ever felt that?"*

"Yes, many times, but anytime I felt down and discouraged, my friend Sharon helped me, as did Nisang Ji, who always encouraged and supported me. Before I was locked here, he cautioned and encouraged me to be brave." Tamanna said this in a hushed tone.

Lakshya paused and questioned Tamanna, *"Are you talking about Nisang ji Maharaj, the priest of that ancient temple in Ajmer."*

"Yes," she said, raising her eyebrows. *"Do you know him?"* she inquired.

"I live in Ajmer," he replied enthusiastically, which made them blush. Also, they had a purpose to be cheerful and motivated. *"This can't be the door for any of us, we both want to live this life so rebirth is not the option, let's go,"* Lakshya said:

The chain of our emotions remains connected, and somewhere we provide meaning to each other's lives. The same thing happened just today between Tamanna and Lakshya. Tamanna starts walking and says, *"I live in Vaishali Nagar, and where do you live?"* *"I stayed in Shastri Nagar,"* Lakshya said. *"Once upon a time, I had made a design to give to my mother but that day she scolds me so much because*

I got 78 marks in the test which was out of 100." Tamanna went on: *"Well, leave it, now perhaps these things do not mean anything because perhaps now we are imprisoned here forever."*

*"No, I don't think so since, look, another door has opened; let's just hope that this one leads us to our planet. So we may go there and tell our parents what we need to do and what will happen if we don't."*Lakshya encouraged her to remain persistent since the outcome was not inevitable.

"Do you think there would be someone looking for us in our world right now?" Tamanna questioned Lakshya.

*"Your parents and friends may be"*responded Lakshya. *"And what about yours you must be having good friends?"* Tamanna inquired, *"Unfortunately, I don't have any friends with whom I can express my feelings. Yes, I have two childhood pals, but they are unaware that I aspire to be a jewelry designer. They may have attempted to find me, but my parents may not have done so yet. I'm a burden to them, right?"* Lakshya was upset, grew sorrowful, and hung his head.

Tamanna's gaze shifts to another door in the distance, this time a silver loom. The Silver Loom: Silver threads formed fascinating patterns in the air. Lakshya's eyes widened.*"It's like my jewelry designs come alive,"*he told Tamanna. The loom symbolized artistry and determination—the fortitude to create beauty despite all circumstances. *"Maybe this door is for you,"* Tamanna replied to Lakshya, looking slightly feeling sad. Lakshya was also wondering that perhaps he had found a way out of there. He didn't want to leave Tamanna there alone. They quickly created a profound relationship. Because they communicated well in a short period and became friends. Perhaps as much as no one has realized till now, there was a long hush between them, as if that empty area had turned barren again. But somebody had to make this decision.

It appears that those two's thinking has been sealed. They couldn't think of anything. But Tamanna responded, *"Go away"* with a heavy heart. *"And what if this door is not for me?"* Lakshya said. *"We had decided that whatever decision will be taken now will be taken after discussion between both of us."* Lakshya continued. *"It is also possible that this is just an illusion or it may start shrinking like before."* Tamanna just kept listening to him, head down, believing that this was the proper thing for him. Tamanna stopped him and said, *"Go, I think this door is probably only for you."* *"How can you say this with such surety?"* Lakshya inquired

Tamanna simply stayed silent without responding, as she lacked a definite explanation but after giving a thought she said *"Okay, let's make a deal, you go in and if the way starts shrinking or anything such happens I will also join you but if you go in and doesn't happen then you have to keep walking through the way."*

Tamanna removed an earring and remarked while embracing Lakshya, *"It is not your dream to assist me. Rather, you aspire to be a famous designer. And consider, if I had discovered something relating to my dream sooner, I would have had to go, wouldn't I?"* Tamanna muttered this, turned her face and began marching forward.

Lakshya started moving in that door and after a while, he was out of sight, in the way he was wondering if Tamanna's estimate was correct and if I went home, she would be left alone there. Maybe this is a dream, and I'll get out. But if the contrary occurs, we will be estranged from each other, and nothing will be accomplished. He was still unsure what to do, but Tamanna did not glance back, so he waited there, pondering what he should do till she was out of sight. He mustered the bravery to enter the door, which he did with fear.

Tamanna was merely going on, wondering whether Lakshya had discovered the entrance to his aspirations. Then, after some contemplation, she realized that perhaps Lakshya had located the appropriate door and had entered the real world. She saw the next door after wandering for a while.

She saw the Crystal Mirror, which signifies reflecting their images, and the symbol of the mirror spoke, *"Know you."* Tamanna touched it and felt her concerns dissolve. *"Courage begins with understanding what we truly are,"* she said. What does it mean to see a mirror? Mirrors represent reflection, and how will I know if it is linked to my passion or not? Tamanna asks herself and recalls Lakshya. I wish Lakshya had been here; it would have been easier for me to grasp. She couldn't comprehend anything, so she sat on a stone for a long time. Suddenly, while sitting, she remembered Nisang ji's comments and began to think.

Nisang ji often talked about bravery. Will I be able to emerge from the dream world alone through my courage? Please assist or provide a clue so that I can comprehend. Maybe if I show myself bravely in the mirror or imagine myself as a famous designer, all of this will cease. I don't think that will happen. I should go on without spending any more time.

Tamanna explained herself and began to move further, until when she noticed a thing approaching her. As Tamanna hesitates, a sweet voice resonates down the corridor. Lyra, an ethereal figure with silver hair and starry eyes, appears. She wears a flowing gown decorated with stars. *"Hi, Tamanna. I'm the Dream Guide. Trust your senses; the symbols indicate more than just beauty. They reflect your heart's desires."* Lyra explained her duty, held her hand, and began to fly up. *"I am only allowed to give you information on how to identify doors, but the choice will be yours only."*

Tamanna questioned Lyra, *"Why have you arrived so late? Where have you been all this time? Everyone expected you to comprehend this, but you never showed up."*

"You are in a world of dreams, so the dreams will work according to your subconscious mind, and so your mind gave me birth just now," Lyra remarked, pointing her finger at the first door that appeared:

The Raven Door (Symbol of Freedom). Behind this door is a big sky, where ravens fly freely. Choosing it represents breaking free of restraints. Tamanna would pursue her creative passion, disregarding her family's desires. Lyra murmurs, *"To fly with the ravens is to reclaim your voice."*

The Crescent Moon Door (a symbol of mystery)**: Beyond this threshold, moonlight woodlands await. Here, secrets and hidden information wait. Choosing it entails solving puzzles and exploring unexpected ways. Lyra says, *"The moon reveals truths hidden in shadows."*

The blooming rose door (a symbol of passion)**: - Behind this door is a thriving garden. Rose's blossom and their petals are aflame. Choosing it represents accepting emotion, even if it goes against reasoning. - Lyra grins, *"The rose blooms despite the thorns." "So can you."*

The Sapphire Bridge: A transparent bridge across a chasm. *"To cross or not?"* Tamanna thought. Lyra told Tamanna that *"the sapphire symbolized trust—the courage to leap, even when the path seemed uncertain."*

The Laurel Crown: Laurel leaves ringed their heads. *"Victory,"* Tamanna muttered. *"Courage isn't just about dreams; it's about claiming our rightful place."* Tamanna nodded, aware of the crown's significance.

The Whispering Oak's old bark had inscriptions. *"Listen,"* Tamanna implored. The oak represented wisdom—the fortitude to seek direction beyond their narrow perceptions.

The Star Map: Constellations danced across the sky. Tamanna tracked Orion's belt. *"Guidance,"* she said. *"We need courage to follow our stars, not the ones our parents set."*

The Golden Quill: Ink streamed from its nib, creating words in midair. *"Write your destiny,"* Tamanna read. The quill represented expression—the fortitude to write their aspirations into reality.

The Dancing Light: A flickering light contained mysteries. *"Passion,"* Tamanna muttered. *"Courage ignites when we embrace what sets our souls on fire."*

The Moonstone Compass: Its luminescence is directed northward. *"Direction,"* Tamanna stated. *"We must find our way, even if it means defying tradition."* The moonstone symbolized intuition—the fortitude to follow their inner compass.

The timeless hourglass: Sand streamed continuously. *"Patience,"* Tamanna moaned. *"Courage isn't always about swift action; sometimes, it's waiting for the right moment."*

Tamanna stares at the symbols, divided between dread and desire. She recalls her abandoned sketchbooks, the songs she secretly murmured, and the colors that were about to break forth.

- Lyra's eyes are full of sympathy. *"Choose, Tamanna. "Your heart knows."*

When you create things in your subconscious mind, your brain often gives you worries linked to them. And as soon as you start thinking about something via your brain, you start making it visible through your brain, and that dread starts to go. As a result, whenever you materialize, do it through your brain rather than storing it in your subconscious. Courage is the only way to conquer any fear.

You constantly let your fear overcome your courage, therefore Ezra imprisoned you in the land of dreams to teach you or make you understand the power of courage. You must study and grow your intellect according to the circumstances. Now battle courageously and see how you will receive hints when you begin manifesting things confidently.

Angels are constantly around, but we cannot see or hear them due to our fear. The power of manifesting things is the only way to get rid of the fear that prevents you from being fearless, and remember that angels do not always come smiling into your life; sometimes, angels have to take various pathways to transform your life and leave.

As they discussed, Tamanna realized that bravery was woven throughout every sign, not just one. They joined hands, and their determination increased. Together, they'd discover the sign that would guide them back to reality, where their hopes awaited fulfillment.

As soon as Tamanna is revealed, these doors reveal our whole adventure. She feared she had lost Lakshay, so she went back to see whether he was still there.

V

Chapter five

Before she could get there, she encountered Lakshya on the way. They raced to each other and hugged. Tamanna began by stating, ***"All of these doors are part of our path; we must pass through them."*** She told Lakshya about Lyra and stated that ***"all the paths we have crossed so far teach us a lesson, and to get out of here, we will have to understand all of these paths properly."***

In her enthusiasm, she neglected to inquire about what happened to Lakshya in the door through which he had gone at her request. Then, keeping her cool, she inquired, ***"What happened to you at that door and how did you come out?"***

Lakshya smiled and added, ***"When I entered this door, all I could see was silver. I was confused for a time, but then I saw it was imprisoning me. By the time it had taken me, I had rushed out the door. What occurred, and what were you telling me? Now, tell me peacefully."***

Tamanna began speaking cautiously, but with a little grin, for she had gotten Lakshya back. ***"I was terribly sad when you went off. And after being alone, I was frustrated, so***

I begged for assistance. Lyra, an angel, appeared. She took off holding my hand and explained the meaning of the symbol above each door. And, certainly, it has been stated that angels do not always appear smiling to organize your life; they may also assist in other ways."

Lakshya asked, **"Great! And did she say something about the route out of here?"**

She responded: **"nothing much but she said that it is your journey and you have to complete it with courage, and yes she said that this is the dream world and it works in the same way as our dreams do, that is, it is associated with our subconscious mind."**

Lakshya remarked, **"Okay, nice! So if we seek for aid, it will deliver some sort of help."**

After a few minutes of thought, he answered, **"Okay!" So from now on, unless we discover any support, we will just focus on that."**

Tamanna answered *"Okay,"* and they both hadn't realized they were holding one other's hands. When Tamanna and Lakshya realized they were holding each other's hands, Tamanna felt bashful and gently pushed her hair out behind her ears. When she did this, Lakshya discovered that her earrings had been altered again, and they were the same pattern he created a few years before. Then he said, **"Have you realized that your earrings have been changed again and this one is again my design that I made years ago."**

She took the earring out of her ears in amazement to examine, and they had been altered. **"How is this happening? "And what does it mean?"**

Lakshya responded: **"I think we are somehow connected and this is happening because it might be possible that we have something in common in the real world"**

After going a mile, they came across an upside-down temple and quickly ran, hoping to find a way out. However, the area is unfamiliar, and it is difficult to grasp what is good and bad for them, as well as what they should and should not do. Tamanna was unsure, so she questioned Lakshya, *"Do you think it will work"*

"Do we have another option?" Lakshya answered, *"Do you want to go back after what your parents did to you on the last day of your 12th-grade exams?"* Lakshya asked Tamanna. She was surprised that I hadn't spoken anything about that day, so she asked *"How do you know about my parents"*

"I don't know them, but before coming here, I saw a movie in Crystal Ball, which Ezra showed. It revealed practically everything about you." Lakshya responded and stopped speaking. *"I asked because I want to solve the mystery behind this frequent changing of your earrings and"*

"and, and what?" Tamanna asked him, but he clutched Tamanna's hand and rushed to find a spot to hide since he saw someone approaching from outside. A guy walked towards the temple with hunched shoulders. When the individual approached, Lakshya exclaimed, *"Uncle,"* referring to Shravan's father. He informed Tamana, *"I know him; he is my friend's father."* Tamanna, concerned, answered, *"Be safe, it could be a trap"* and remained hidden.

He called out, *"Hello, uncle,"* but he was terrified since he didn't know if he was genuine or if it was all a trick. Mr. Sharma turned to face him and said, *"Hello! "Beta,"* *"Uncle, what brought you here?* When Uncle saw him, he said, *"Lakshya, you made it here."* I had expected you to visit us at some point. I am running out of time, so let me tell you that you are still in phase one of your dream. Stay strong and find the door with a symbol of Vishnu ji; it is the only* *door from which you can get out of here. And during your journey in the dream world, stay away from the whispers of evil spirits,"* He proceeded to stroll in the direction of the upside-down temple door.

"How do you know this much about this place?" inquired Lakshya.

Tamanna and Lakshya followed Mr. Sharma as he stated, *"Come with me, I'll show you something,"* and they both opened the temple's door to discover thousands of people chained in iron chains performing something. They both were terrified, and Tamanna began screaming, *"What the hell is that, we won't be able to go back to our world."* and started wailing on Lakshya's shoulders. Lakshya grabs her and says, *"We are seeing this because of our subconscious mind, maybe."* After keeping her calm for a time, they both enquired as to *"who they were." "These are the spirits of all the ones who suffered their dreams, some for their family, some for money, each of them has their own story,"* Mr. Sharma continued to walk.

"Uncle, tell me why you are here and not bound like they are." Lakshya enquired

Mr. Sharma invited them in and said, *"Come, let me show you something."* He then led them to the basement. Once more, everything was over in a brand-new universe where everyone was engaged in various creative endeavors, like writing, painting, and instrument playing.

Inquiring, *"Who are they?"* Lakshya

"They are the ones who are still following their dreams but as a hobby," Mr. Sharma said. *"Take careful note of each of them. They are bent over. In actuality, it was all of them who gave up on their goal in favor of a job. They all came here and went there because they were passionate about what they were doing, even if they all had some sort of duty. However,*

none of them is happy with what they are doing at the moment."

Tamanna and Lakshya both scowled and were depressed. *"Do you know where we will find that Vishnu Ji's sign door?"* inquired Tamanna. *"It's hard to say because I haven't been there, but I know someone who is quite knowledgeable about this site; folks call him BABA, and he is generally spotted in the northeast. Now that Ezra has given you both a time limit, you both have a limited amount of time to find him."*

They both began to realize what may be at the northeast of this location when he shoved them both and began to go back to his target. *"Those who can fight for themselves can win,"* Lakshya recalled, *"but even God cannot help those who accept everything before the fight."* Mr. Sharma added, *"So fight, your destiny is in your hands now,"* and then he disappeared.

"What should we do now?" Tamanna enquired. *"Let's fight,"* Lakshya said, and they began to move towards one other. Luckily, he was carrying a watch with a compass, so they decided to follow it and headed towards the northeastern region of that desolate area.

Tamanna questioned, *"Back there, you were saying something that you know about me and all,"* after they had been traveling for a minute towards the northeast. *"However, I am unaware of your background. What is your story?"* *"When I was twelve years old, I created my first design, which I sent to my mother. I didn't receive any praise for it, instead, my parents gave me a lot of reprimands—my father even slapped me—and told me that everything I had designed was linked to girls."* Lakshya shed a few tears as he was speaking.

Tamanna comforted Lakshya by placing her hand on his shoulder and saying, ***"It's okay if you don't want to continue."***

"No, I want to tell everyone everything about myself because I haven't had a chance to express my feelings to anyone yet." After saying this, Lakshya carried on with the tale. ***"That's when I realized that I like the feel of silk over boys' shirts and trousers. I've made a lot of new drawings up to this point, but I've never been able to show them to anyone."*** ***"Can you hear something?"*** Tamanna said, gesturing with her palm to her ear as she stopped him. ***"No,"*** Lakshya answered.

Tamanna began to move a little faster toward the sound while still holding Lakshya's hand. When she heard the sound clearly, Lakshya said, ***"Yes, it's raining somewhere."*** Tamanna became excited and began running in that direction, but Lakshya became a little concerned because they were in a dream world and nothing normal had happened up until that point. He warned Tamanna to be careful because they were not on Earth and that everything that happened here had a reason.

However, Tamanna does not want to hear any of the cautions that Lakshya was saying since she has always wanted to enjoy the rain and was denied the opportunity, which is why she had never experienced this till now. All she wanted to do was enjoy the rain without paying attention to anything. Rain was falling in a tiny region, and she could not stop herself from running ahead. She was very happy to see those raindrops; they seemed like a huge gift. She grabbed Lakshya's hand and began dancing in the rain. Right now, her delight had no bounds. Lakshya continued to enjoy the rain with her without saying anything. As the rain continued to pour down, Lakshya couldn't help but think how much she wanted this adventure to conclude so she could finally meet and get to know Tamanna in person. Tamanna beckoned Lakshya with a gesture after a while when she noticed him standing by the side. Even Lakshya became enthralled by Tamanna and began dancing in the rain.

After a considerable amount of time, Lakshya took Tamanna's hand and said, *"We have to keep moving forward."* Tamanna made a mournful look and, despite her want to, they both began walking away from that location. *"Remember what Uncle Sharma said. We are here for a specific period and we have to find our way within that period,"* Lakshya stated. Tamanna turned to hastily dry her hair, and her hair fell squarely upon Lakshya's face. After apologizing, Tamanna questioned, *"Didn't you like it?"*

"Is that your hair falling straight on my face?" Lakshya teased Tamanna with this in a lighthearted manner.

"Oh no, dear, I was talking about rain," she said, turning her face away as she began to move and gather her hair. They were silent for a while; maybe they both wanted to say something, but many feelings are best expressed without words.

"Hey! You are an excellent dancer." Lakshya said

Tamanna had never expressed her sentiments to anybody before, so she was feeling rather uncomfortable. *"You know, when I was a tiny child, my mother warned me not to go outside and play with Sharon since it was pouring. After that, I told my mother I had to go, just as any other child would. You know what my mother did? She locked me in the room and gave me two slaps. I've been terrified of the rain ever since. What's even more astonishing is that I no longer fear my mother; yet, following that day, I developed a fear of rain in the shadow. I used to shut the room's gates and windows as soon as it started to rain. I apologize if I upset you, but I just forgot where I was today when I had a chance."*

"Hey!" What is the reason for your apology?" Lakshya interrupted her, took her hand, and said, *"Stop it, you are free here with me so chill and relax now we must keep moving forward."* He then began to walk quickly. *"What makes us run?"* Taking deep breaths, Tamanna questioned. *"Because I want to leave this place as soon as possible, meet you, and realize my dreams."* Tamanna questioned, *"What are you hiding, please share?"* she released both of his hands after noticing that Lakshya was wearing an odd expression. Turning around, Tamanna stated to Lakshya, *"Look, there is no one here to judge us or stop us."*

Lakshya lost all self-control, broke down in tears, and added, *"I've always wanted a friend like you—someone who understands and doesn't judge me."*

Tamanna grabs Lakshya's hand and moves in its direction as soon as they hear someone laughing loudly. They notice a pair sitting there, their hands clasped together. Lakshya wipes away his tears and begins examining them closely. Tamanna stares at them first and then grins as she looks at Lakshya. *"Why is the couple just laughing while they sit there?"* Tamanna poses an important question to Lakshya. Lakshya simply shrugs his shoulders and makes an expression that suggests he is equally perplexed. *"Let's go inquire,"* says Tamanna. Lakshya nods and accompanies Tamanna there.

"Hi there! Are the two of you stuck here with us as well?" With hesitation, Tamanna asks them. The unidentified youngster assures the pair, *"No, we both come here of our own free will,"* as they glance at Tamanna and Lakshya. *"We've been visiting this place for a very long time."*

"Is there anything else you can tell us about this place or how to leave?" Lakshya asks in a hopeful tone.

"No, we just met here and my Revathi doesn't exist in the real world. We don't know much about this place." In response, the boy gestures to the female seated next to him. *"I couldn't understand,"* Tamanna asks.

"This is Revathi, and my name is Suraj. We only met in a dream. I was having some family issues one day when all of a sudden, Revathi appeared to me in a dream. She took my hand and guided me to this wonderful place where we may both live. And eventually, everything comes to an end, and I have to return to the world where my people hate me." After responding, Suraj says, *"What about you guys?"* to both of them.

"My name is Tamanna and he is Lakshya, and we are stuck here in the dream world," Tamanna says, introducing herself and Lakshya. Lakshya asks, *"If you don't mind, I would like to know your story,"* as he gives Suraj a curious glance. Tamanna gives Lakshya a sidelong glance before motioning for us to leave them alone. With excitement, Suraj asks, *"Why not sit?"*

"I met Revathi about 160 years ago in Agra," Suraj continues, putting his hand on hers. Revathi, a foreigner, traveled to India with her family under the British Raj. We initially met at the temple of Ambey Mata. The sun was so hot that he could hardly feel his feet, and a robber had stolen her shoes from outside the temple. I hand her my slippers after that. Her companions started laughing but she did not respond to their laughter; instead, she slipped on my slippers, said "thank you," and walked away. The next day, she returned my slippers by herself to Mata's temple.

Her name was Emma in those days. We fell in love and we saw each other almost every day after that. I called her Revathi since I didn't like the name Emma. It's time for her to head back to England now that our love has blossomed. We both informed our parents about it, but her family sent her back to England when they rejected our explanations. We stopped communicating because we did not have any source to communicate with each other and I got married in India because of my parent's pressure.

She never got married, but she loved me so much that she's been looking for me ever since. However, we were never able to get into contact. But one day I dreamed that we met paths in this dream world dimension. She has held my hand ever since to console me on difficult days. When we are together, we are in a zone that is off-limits to outsiders."

Revathi and Suraj vanished out of nowhere just after that.

"If we can never be happy when we return to our world, will you come back here with me?" Tamanna pleaded, taking Lakshya by the hand.

"Indeed!" Lakshya hugged Tamanna after saying, **"But I promise you that I will never let this happen. I don't know about you, but I will never stop fighting for you until you reach your goal."** Tamanna seemed slightly distressed upon realizing that she still lacks bravery, but she also experienced delight at knowing that someone is now concerned for her well-being and that they will stand up for her anytime she feels weak.

We must have the support of others to remain brave and cheerful, regardless of our desire for it, since no matter what, you can always count on someone to be there for you when you need them.

Lakshya was asked by Tamanna, who held out her hand, **"Will you promise that you will never leave me?"** **"I will not leave you alone as long as I have breath,"** Lakshya said, putting his hand on hers showing concern. They hug each other and begin walking in search of the baba that can help them leave this place, saying, ***"At this world or any world we will stay together forever."*** Lakshya moved ahead.

After going for a mile, they came to a temple, but upon arriving they saw that not only was the building upside down but there was also a banyan tree, which was hanging upside down in midair. ***"I know this place; it is where I always used to go; it is near to my place; it is where I met Nisang Ji who always encouraged me to confront my fear,"*** Tamanna said, glancing at the temple. She then began running in its direction and discovered an upside-down baba hanging beneath the hanging banyan tree. ***"Is that you, Nisang Ji?"*** she inquired.

"Indeed! It's me, Tamanna. As I mentioned before, the time has arrived for you to muster your bravery." After saying this and directing them to ***"come out of there by jumping into the temple as the gates are going to close soon,"*** Nisang Ji left them searching everywhere for the gate. Finally, Tamana showed Lakshya where the gate was—at the top of the temple, where a symbol representing Vishnu ji's statue is located—so they both leaped through it while holding hands.

VI
Chapter six

"Mummy," a child calling her mother from a room where she is sleeping while clutching a blanket, said in a far-off voice. When her mother arrived, Tamanna—who had grown up and wed Lakshya—was there. Sanaya is a little ball of activity, with sparkling eyes and a contagious smile. Even at the age of eight, her love of dancing is as intense as the sun's warmth. Her deft feet dance over the floor, telling tales with each elegant step. Whether doing a vibrant Bollywood dance or a traditional ballet, Sanaya's energy is contagious as she spins and jumps. Her best times are the moments when she is engulfed in music, submerged in the beat, and transformed into a happy rainbow.

"Sanaya, what happened?" Tamanna said, **"I'm in the middle of something, just get up, it's time to go school,"**and she resumed drawing designs on paper. She has grown to be a very well-known designer in the field, and both Tamana and Lakshya have positions in it and successfully manage businesses under the name Sanaya Creations.

After wiping her eyes, Sanaya exits her room, settles down on the couch, and declares, **"I don't want to go to** *school today!"*

She said calmly, *"Why, what's the reason?"* to which Sanaya answered, *"Because my best friend Udita is not coming to school."*

"This is not a good reason, go get ready or find some other reason," Tamnna remarked while drawing a sketch.

"Arey! I don't want to go to school because Udita's mother is too strict and won't let her play badminton, even though she's talented at the game and has even stated that she wants to play badminton like Saina Nehwal." She expressed this while breaking down in tears for Udita.

Tamanna questioned Sanaya, *"Why isn't she coming to school then?"* *"Her mother scolded her for playing badminton and receiving a certificate yesterday."* Sanaya replied *"That's good, her mother should be happy then,"* Tamanna retorted Seeking information, Sanaya said, *"Exactly! However, she received an 80 out of 100 on her test",* so Sanaya hurried inside her mother's room after saying this.

Tamanna asked Lakshya over the phone to pick up a present wrap from the market when he got home tonight. She informed Lakshya what Sanaya had said about Udita that morning when he returned from his workplace. Then she got up, wrapped a book as a present, and they both called for Sanaya to come out. Presenting the gift-wrapped book to Sanaya, they called her out to the living room and said, *"This is for Udita and her parents. Give it to her in school tomorrow and tell her we sent it for their parents"*

The following morning, Sanya hurriedly dressed for school as she wanted to offer that gift to her. *"My mum has sent this gift for your mum and dad,"* she remarked as she gave Udita the gift.

"What is it?" inquired Udita. *"It seems like a book or something."* You just deliver it to your parents. *"Lead the*

way to the assembly hall, please we are getting late."

"Sanaya's mother gave this to you," Udita remarked as she handed the book to her mother when she reached home later that day.

When she unwrapped the present, she discovered a book with the words **"Dare To Dream"** printed on the cover page. She begins to read the book, which tells Tamanna and Lakshya's narrative. When she reached the part in the novel where Tamanna and Lakshya managed to get out of that dream world, she was reading it and didn't even realize it was becoming dark outside. Unexpectedly, Udita's father has returned from his workplace when the doorbell rings. Up to the moment they were able to leave that dream world, she tells Udita's father the entire tale.

With excitement, Udita's father inquires, *"What happened after that?"*

"You freshen up, I'll prepare food and finish it at night before sleeping," Udita's mother suggested. *"However, I need to do something crucial first."* Having said this, she walks to Udita's room and gives her a strong hug. She simply gave her hugs and kisses without saying anything further and then returned to the kitchen to start cooking.

That novel is still being read at night by Udita's parents. So they had their dinner earlier than usual at around 8 PM and her mother asked Udita to go to bed early tonight. So, Udita and her parents went to their respective rooms and they both started reading from the point her mother left the mysterious tale of Tamanna and Lakshya.

Tamanna had just gotten out of her dream and found herself in the hospital she questioned the nurse standing next to her *"Where am I?"*

"You are in a hospital, beta. Keep yourself calm you are safe now" The nurse held her back as she was trying to get

her consciousness back and wanted to sit. She enquired about her parents *"Where my parents are, and why they are not here with me"*

"Your father just went to the pharmacy a minute ago" the nurse replied.

"Were they worried?" she asked and got a little worried.

"Yes! But it is strange being a doctor he was not able to diagnose what has happened to you." The nurse said and picked up the bottle of glucose.

"I am calling sir, you just relax you are still weak, don't get up," the nurse told Tamanna and left her in the room alone.

Before she could think of anything about what happened Sharon came into the room and said *"thank god, you are alive."*

Tamanna, still perplexed by what has transpired, asks Sharon, *"Haven't you gone to Mumbai?"*

"Mumbai, why would I go to Mumbai?" Sharon replied

Tamanna gathered herself and asked Sharon *"How did I come here and what happened to me?"*

"you were in this state of unconsciousness for the last two days since we have given our last exam of 12th grade, that day your parents scolded you for making designs" Sharon quickly told him everything and said, *"Now you have regained consciousness and I told everything to my father. Now you also gather some courage and say everything to your mother and father. Remember me and my father is always with you."*

Tamanna just kept quiet and listened to Sharon and kept wondering whether what she saw in that dream world was true. Before she could understand anything, her parents came there. Tamanna and Sharon both get cringed for a second. Tamanna's mother started crying and came running and as soon as she bent down to hug her, Tamanna said *"I **don't want to be a doctor; I want to be a fashion designer. My sketches are not just normal papers that should just be thrown in the dustbin they are my dreams and I will follow my passion and accomplish my dream to be a fashion designer whether you stay with me in my journey or not one day I will become a famous designer."***Tamanna's mother stopped hugging her and stepped back a little because rebellion was visible in Tamanna's voice.

Tamanna's daddy held her mother by the shoulder turned her to the side and said ***"Do whatever you want; we both will never force you to become a doctor."*** and started crying.

Hearing this, Sharon looked at Tamanna and Tamanna looked at Sharon and a slight smile appeared on the faces of both of them. There was a complete silence in that room for a longer period than usual and to break the ice Sharon took the initiative and said ***"Can I spend some time with her alone."***

Tamanna's mother responded to that and said ***"Yes why not, but let her come home first"***

No one can help us unless we help ourselves, Sharon and Nisang Ji tried many times to understand this thing but Tamanna's fear never let her move ahead and fight for her passion. Living a happy life requires having a dream. Dreams offer us direction and a feeling of purpose—something to aim for. They serve as compass points, lighting our way throughout the wide universe. Visualize a ship that has nowhere to go but wanders endlessly. In the same vein, life lacks direction and purpose without dreams. Dreams give us the compass that directs us towards worthwhile objectives. Dreams are strong sources of inspiration. They push us to step beyond our comfort zones and kindle the fire within us. Dreams provide us a glimpse of a better existence, one that is happy, fulfilling, and has a purpose.

Think of a budding artist who dreams of creating masterpieces or an aspiring entrepreneur with visions of transforming industries. These dreams propel them forward, even when obstacles loom large. Fear is the shadow that walks beside our hopes. Fear envelops us in a cocoon of uncertainty, whispering uncertainties and worst-case scenarios. Obstacles appear the jagged ascent up the success mountain, the rushing river of self-doubt, and the prickly thickets of failures. These obstacles get magnified by fear and appear insurmountable.

Fear and dreams dance in the cosmos. Fear draws us back into the security of the known, while our aspirations draw us toward the light. The magic, though, is this: Fearlessness gracefully enters the stage. Despite shaky knees, it whispers, "Leap!" It prods us to accept vulnerability, dance with ambiguity, and face our anxieties. Every step we take towards our goals is a rejection of fear—a statement that our ambitions are more important than our uncertainties.

Dreams help us become resilient. Dreams moor us while storms roar. We adjust to the winds of change, bending but not breaking. Think of the rejected writer, the unsuccessful scientist, or the musician who practices through the night. Their dreams provide them strength and inspire them to revise, reassess, and practice. Dreams are the creators of change. They map out our development, suggesting ways to traverse fear-filled gaps. The melodies of our dreams come together to form a symphony, a harmonic whole. Every dream counts, whether it's mumbled in a child's prayer before bed or engraved in an elderly person's wrinkles. Honouring our dreams is a part of adding to this symphony.

We enrich the earth for future generations by including hints of potential, resiliency, and hope.

A few months later, Tamanna's result came out, and she passed with 94 per cent, but now she had the freedom to fulfill her dreams, to become something on her hard work and grit. Today is the first day of college, and Tamanna has beautifully designed a gorgeous red top. She was coming out of the corridor very happy after attending the first lecture but she bumped into a boy who was coming from the other side who was also happy to attend the lecture. Both of their files fell to the ground when they were picking up each other's sketches, and at the same time, both their hands landed on the same picture, which was not a design but a picture of a person that was in of their files, it was Ezra's picture.

"Tamanna" and "Lakshya," they both say in the same tone and with the same excitement.

Both of them went and sat under a tree and Tamanna held the hand of Lakshya and asked **"What happened with you when we left the dream world?"**

Lakshya took a deep breath and said in response to Tamanna's words.

"Eternity blended into two days. I was lying in a hospital room when I opened my eyes. My parents worriedly stood there, furrowing their brows. My mother said, "Lakshya, you were unconscious." We discovered you surrounded by drawings on the couch.

My father became less severe. "Son, you were losing your heartbeats?"

I paused before talking about jungles of gemstones and rivers of silver. I said out loud that I wanted to be a jewellery designer rather than an engineer. My words hung there, as delicate as petals caressed by dew.

My mum gave me a cheek pad. "Lakshya, our fantasies are like sarees. There are bright silks and delicate cottons among them. Yours is a jewel-filled tapestry.

My dad let out a sigh. Maybe we haven't seen it. Your compass is your passion. My kid makes jewellery. We'll patch things up with your dreams.

I have then woven my way along. The crimson silk of the saree, which spoke boldness, became my inspiration. I enrolled at this college to study gemmology, worked as an apprentice for skilled artisans, and produced jewellery that was worn by both commoners and queens.

The sofa changed my destiny in the Verma home. The drawings, the silk, and the youngster who dared to dream were all imprinted with dreams. As I wove gold and silver, my parents' emotions softened into acceptance."

They both were sitting holding each other hand for an hour and since then they have been supporting each other till today. Tamanna was a fashion designer whose boutique on a street glistened like a misplaced gem, while Lakshya's name is a byword for classic elegance. Their creations glisten in the windows of upscale stores, decorate royal necks, and grace red carpets. Their steadfast passion and the enchantment they weave with each piece, gemstone, and exquisite thread are evident in every piece they produce.

When her father came home from work the next day, he had a gift for her: a set of badminton rackets. *"For the premier Ajmer academy,"* he stated, passing the application to Udita. *"You deserve wings for your dreams."*

While all of this was going on, Nisang Ji knelt down to take Udita's rain soaked photo from the Terries. Straightening up, he cast a shadow that reflected the shape of Ezra, the mysterious guy who had led Tamanna and

Lakshya through their dream world.

Maybe there was something hidden under Nisang Ji's shadow, a gateway to a world where dreams and reality collided. And when the rain swept away the old beliefs, new opportunities appeared like monsoon flowers, promising a time in the future when bravery and desire would be king.

Epilogue

Now, let's explore this fascinating epilogue from the fictional novel **"Dare to Dream"**.

Beyond imagination, the dream realm had mysteries where bravery was put to the test and reality became hazy. Two unsuspecting people, Tamanna and Lakshya, became imprisoned behind its strange walls. Their path was marked by determination, affection, and rebellion.

With her untamed soul, Tamanna tackled the puzzles that the old banyan tree told to her. With every response, she got one step closer to solving the secrets of the dream world.

Cognizant and practical, Lakshya interpreted symbols carved into the fabric of the dream. His fanciful universe contrasted with his technical intellect.

They found what is said to be the **Path of Lumina**, a route that leads back to reality. However, it was prohibited. Their concerns gave the dream world fuel, and it also fed off their desire for independence.

The expectations of their parents were quite important. Tamanna's parents pushed for her to become a doctor, whereas Lakshya's parents expected him to flourish in engineering.

Tamanna clasped Lakshya's hand and felt her heart race. She said, "We can't stay here forever." "Our dreams are waiting." Lakshya's mouth clenched. "However, our parents," Tamanna interjected, "Our dreams matter too." "We'll find a way." The Path of Lumina glistened, a gateway between dimensions. Stepping on top of the ancient temple hanging upside down, Tamanna felt her heart quicken. Lakshya paused. "What if we fail?"

"I swear we won't," she said. "Together." Dreamworld memories, uncertainties, and illusions battled back. Lakshya's wrench gleamed, and Tamanna's stethoscope appeared. A ghostly voice said, "Choose." "Doctor or engineer?" The emblems were abandoned. "None," they said. "We choose us." Tamanna and Lakshya staggered into reality as dawn opened. Their parents waited, duty and desires at odds. "We're artists," Tamanna declared. "Dreamers." Lakshya smiled. "And we'll build our own world." Dream echoes trailing behind, Tamanna and Lakshya went out into the bright dawn. Their bravery had created a new route where emotion took victory over convention.

May their narrative encourage others to follow their aspirations despite all challenges?

Afterword: "Dare To Dream"

In the quiet corners of our classrooms, where textbooks rustle and calculators hum, there is a subtle rebellion—a protest against the strict boundaries of traditional achievement. It's a rebellion headed by visionaries, artists, and those who dare to draw outside the lines.

Her eyes contained universes, and I saw her as I sat in the school auditorium surrounded by nervous parents and perfectly ironed uniforms. She didn't fit the mould, and I can't say who she is. Her heart was beating to a different beat than the worries of those who worried about periodic tables and quadratic equations. Her dream was to work as a fashion designer.

Like many others, her parents were devout followers of the high grades. Success was evaluated by percentages rather than by sentiments. However, her dreams were made of sequins and silk, not algebraic equations. Entering her mother's wardrobe surreptitiously, she would wrap herself in sarees and spin around like a Bollywood star. She stroked the cloth, which her parents thought unimportant, and her eyes lit up.

The school declared a cultural tournament one day. "Tradition and Modernity" is the topic. It was a bold concept she had. She would dress in a saree made of her mother's red silk, not just any saree. She would let her aspirations unfold, dispel preconceptions, and challenge expectations.

She stood erect, the folds of her saree whispering secrets as the stage lights illuminated her. The crowd let out a gasp. Parents looked at each other. But she moved, her stride resounding with bravery. She was expressing her reality via her saree, not simply covering it up.

The boundaries between tradition and revolt were blurred by her performance. Her laughter reverberated along the hallway as she whirled. The judges were undecided if this was art or defiance. But the cheers became louder, overpowering any scepticism. Because she had the audacity to dream, she instantly became a lighthouse for all suppressed passions.

Her performance stirred discussions. Parents questioned what they had expected of them. Instructors revised their grading schemes. A child who preferred drawing to doing equations sensed a change in the audience. He could not just be a student but also an artist.

Though she was not the competition winner, she did win hearts. As her parents saw the fire in their daughter's eyes, they became softer. That youngster founded a covert art group where colours were used in place of calculations. And me? I used her sari resistance into the writing of this tale.

So, dear reader, whenever you're feeling suffocated by expectations, remember the girl and the boy. Dare to dream, even if it means donning a saree among an ocean of uniforms. For within those folds is a revolution—the type that transforms not just people, but entire worlds.

And when the last curtain closes, may your aspirations speak louder than any report card ever could.